DETECTIVE PAW OF THE LAW

The Case of Piggy's Bank

Time to Read™ is an early reader program designed to guide children to literacy success regardless of age or grade level. The program's three levels correspond to stages of reading readiness, making book selection straightforward, and assuring that when it's time for a child to read, the right book is waiting.

Level 1 — **Beginning to Read**
- Large, simple type
- Basic vocabulary
- Word repetition
- Strong illustration support

Level 2 — **Reading with Help**
- Short sentences
- Engaging stories
- Simple dialogue
- Illustration support

Level 3 — **Reading Independently**
- Longer sentences
- Harder words
- Short paragraphs
- Increased story complexity

DETECTIVE PAW OF THE LAW

The Case of Piggy's Bank

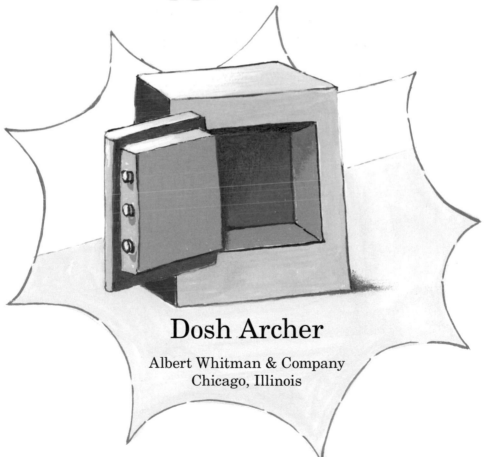

Dosh Archer

Albert Whitman & Company
Chicago, Illinois

To Sylviee

Library of Congress Cataloging-in-Publication data
is on file with the publisher.

Text and illustrations copyright © 2018 by Dosh Archer
Hardcover edition first published in the United States of America
in 2018 by Albert Whitman & Company
Paperback edition first published in the United States of America
in 2019 by Albert Whitman & Company
ISBN 978-0-8075-1564-8

Printed in China
10 9 8 7 6 5 4 3 2 1 WKT 24 23 22 21 20 19

For more information about Albert Whitman & Company,
visit our website at www.albertwhitman.com.

100 Years of Albert Whitman & Company
Celebrate with us in 2019!

Prologue

In the heart of Big City is Big City Police Headquarters, home to the Big City Police Force.

This is where Detective Paw works with his assistant, Patrol Officer Prickles.

Sharp-eyed and straight-talking, Detective Paw can outthink any criminal with his brilliant brain.

Patrol Officer Prickles is brave and loyal and has all the latest police-issue crime-fighting gadgets. He is always there to help Detective Paw.

Together they solve crime; that's what they both love doing…although it's not always easy.

Chapter One

It was early on Monday morning at Big City Police Headquarters.

Detective Paw was just about to bite into his doughnut when his phone rang.

It was Patrol Officer Prickles.

"It's Patrol Officer Prickles here! There has been a robbery at Piggy's Bank. Can you get here as quickly as possible to solve the crime and find the robber?"

"Secure the scene, Prickles," said Detective Paw. "I am on my way."

Detective Paw left his doughnut uneaten, grabbed his notebook and pencil (for writing down clues) and his magnifying glass (for spotting teeny-tiny clues), and leapt into his

Vintagemobile. He put the blue flashy light on the top and sped to the scene of the crime.

When he arrived at the bank, he noticed there was a big, shiny, brand-new Porke power car with the license plate "PIGGY 1" parked right outside.

Patrol Officer Prickles was waiting for him inside the bank. "The scene is secure, sir," he said.

"Well done, Prickles," said Detective Paw. "Let me know what you've got."

Patrol Officer Prickles took out his latest police-issue electronic notepad.

"I arrived at the scene of the crime at 9:04 a.m. I was responding to a call from Piggy the bank manager. He called to say the bank had been broken into. I noticed the following things:

1. The side window was broken.

2. The safe door was open.

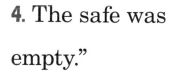

3. There was a crowbar on the floor.

4. The safe was empty."

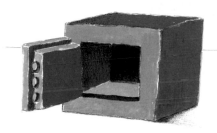

"Well done, Prickles," said Detective Paw. "Good work."

Piggy the bank manager rolled his eyes. "I was the first one here this morning. Someone must have smashed the window, jumped in, broken open the safe, and made off with the money!" Piggy made his eyes go wide. "IT MUST HAVE BEEN A BIG, SCARY ROBBER!" he said.

The rest of the staff gathered around the empty safe. There was Dorothea the cashier and Stanley the security guard.

Dorothea the cashier gasped. "Mrs. Battersbee's life savings! Poor old lady! She's one-hundred-and-one! She was in the bank last thing on Friday. She came in and left her life savings in our care, and now every single penny is gone!"

"Poor Mrs. Battersbee!" said Stanley the security guard. "She is a friend of my mom. She's a really nice lady. I don't know how this could have happened!"

Patrol Officer Prickles looked at Detective Paw.

Detective Paw twiddled his mustache
and popped a peppermint into his
mouth to help him think.

"Everyone calm down," he said. "I will
get to the bottom of this."

Chapter Two

Detective Paw went over to the broken window and looked at the sidewalk outside. He took out his notebook and pencil and made some notes. "Hmm," he said. "That sure is interesting for my investigation."

Patrol Officer Prickles took some photographs of the window with his

latest police-issue camera. He looked at the photos and scratched his head. "What can it all mean?" he asked Detective Paw.

Detective Paw twiddled his mustache. "The broken glass from the window is lying outside on the sidewalk. That means the window was broken from the inside and not the outside." He turned around to speak to everyone.

"The evidence shows whoever did this was perfectly able to get into the bank, without having to break in at all."

There was a long silence and a lot of
uncomfortable looks.

"Who has keys to the bank?" asked
Detective Paw.

"Why, we all do!" cried Dorothea.

"Then that means," said Detective Paw, "the person who stole the money IS IN THIS ROOM!"

"But we are all good people!" cried
Dorothea.

"With all due respect, ma'am," said
Detective Paw, "that remains to be seen."

Chapter Three

"I will need to speak with each one of you and find out where you were this weekend," said Detective Paw. "Dorothea the cashier, I will start with you."

"I was at a spelling bee all weekend," said Dorothea. "I came in second place. I didn't know how to spell 'bumfuzzle.'"

"I hope you have learned how to spell it now," said Detective Paw.

"Yes, sir," said Dorothea.

"I went straight home on Friday night," said Stanley. "To my room, to work on my model airplane. I live with my mom—she'll tell you it's true; she kept bringing me hot chocolate. I took all weekend to build it. It's nearly finished." He pulled out his phone and showed Detective Paw a photograph of

his model P-65 Thunderblast.

"Very nice," said Detective Paw.

Detective Paw fixed his gaze on
Piggy.

"What did you do this weekend?" he
asked him.

Piggy rolled his eyes and pulled out a
peanut butter cup from his pocket and
munched on it. He mumbled something

and some crumbs fell out of his mouth and onto the floor.

"It is very rude to speak with your mouth full," said Detective Paw. "And you haven't answered my question. What did you do this weekend?"

"I went flying," said Piggy, finishing off the peanut butter cup and licking

his lips. "In my new airplane. A real airplane, that is, not a *model* one."

"Gosh," said Stanley. "A real airplane. Wow!"

Detective Paw scratched his head. "Patrol Officer Prickles and I need to talk," he said. "I want everyone to go into the other room."

They all went into the other room.

"Hmm," said Detective Paw. "One of them is lying, but *which* one? This is a two-peppermint problem." Detective Paw popped *another* peppermint into his mouth to help him think extra hard.

After he had thought extra hard, he said, "That Piggy seems a bit too big for his boots. I have a feeling there is something else we need to discover."

"Right," said Patrol Officer Prickles.

Detective Paw started looking around the room again with his magnifying glass.

Patrol Officer Prickles took out
his latest police-issue super-powered
flashlight and looked under the rug and
in all the dark corners. He could see
very well using the flashlight, but he
didn't find any clues.

"Aha!" said Detective Paw. "Look,
Prickles! Marks on the safe door but
NO marks on the safe lock!"

Detective Paw looked even more closely at the lock through his magnifying glass. "That means," said Detective Paw, "this safe was opened! Someone left that crowbar on the floor to make us think it was broken into! Whoever did this knows the secret combination."

Patrol Officer Prickles took a photograph of the safe lock with his latest police-issue camera for evidence.

"Wait a minute," said Detective Paw, taking out his magnifying glass. He had spotted something else, some teeny-tiny stuff just inside the safe.

"Look at this, Prickles," said Detective Paw. "I think this could be our most important clue yet."

Chapter Four

"What is it?" asked Patrol Officer Prickles.

"CRUMBS!" said Detective Paw. "From a peanut butter cup!"

"Prickles," said Detective Paw, opening his notebook. "Let's go over everything we know so far.

1. The window and safe were not broken

into. Whoever did this has keys to the bank and the combination number for the safe.

2. A lot of money was stolen, and Piggy has a new airplane and a new car.

3. I found peanut butter cup crumbs inside the safe, and Piggy eats—"

"Peanut butter cups!" said Patrol Officer Prickles.

"Exactly," said Detective Paw. "I think I know who our criminal is. Let's get them all back in."

Everyone stood in front of Detective Paw and Patrol Officer Prickles.

Detective Paw pointed to the safe.

"Is it true that you, Piggy, are the only one—being the very important manager of this bank, the head person—the only one who has the combination number to the safe?"

Piggy puffed up his chest. He loved feeling important. "Why, yes!" he said. "I am a very important person!"

Detective Paw gave Piggy a very hard stare. "Then can you explain why the safe was opened and not broken into? And why I found peanut butter cup crumbs inside the safe? And how you've been able to buy a brand-new car and an airplane?"

Piggy clamped his trotters over his mouth as he realized he had been outsmarted.

He leapt up and made a dash out the
door, toward his car, with Patrol Officer
Prickles in hot pursuit.

Piggy was fast, but Patrol Officer Prickles was faster.

"Quick, Prickles," shouted Detective Paw. "Don't let him get to his car, or we'll lose him!"

Piggy grabbed his car door handle, but Patrol Officer Prickles lunged, caught Piggy by the back trotters, and brought him down. Piggy wriggled and jiggled, but Patrol Officer Prickles was wearing his latest police-issue EXZ strong-grip gloves, and Piggy could not escape!

"Good work, Prickles," said Detective Paw. He took hold of Piggy and marched him back into the bank so fast his trotters didn't even touch the ground.

"We know it was you," said Detective Paw.

"But why, Piggy, why?" cried Dorothea. "I'm bumfuzzled! You have enough money! You are the manager of a bank! We all trusted you! Mrs. Battersbee trusted you! And she is one-hundred-and-one years old!"

Piggy sneered. "You can never have

enough money, but none of you would understand that. I was fed up with just one house and one car and one swimming pool. I wanted more. I got a new Porke power car and an airplane and a mansion and a flat-screen television and a lifetime supply of peanut butter cups, and I could have gotten away with it if it wasn't for these two troublesome cops." He glared at Detective Paw and Patrol Officer Prickles.

"So there was no robber?" asked
Stanley.

"No, Stanley," said Detective Paw.
"Piggy stayed behind on Friday after
you left. First he smashed the window
to make it look like someone had broken
in, then he used the crowbar to bash
the safe to make it look like it had been

broken open. As well as being a greedy thief, Piggy here is also a LIAR."

Detective Paw turned to Piggy. "It is very bad," said Detective Paw, "to steal when you are meant to be looking after people's money, and it is extremely bad to tell lies. You are a very greedy piggy, and now your lies have caught you out!"

Patrol Officer Prickles clamped a pair of the latest police-issue EXZ steel handcuffs on Piggy. "Try getting out of those," he said.

Outside the bank a crowd had
gathered. They had seen the police
cars and heard all the money had been
stolen from the bank. When Patrol
Officer Prickles marched Piggy outside,
Mrs. Battersbee pushed her way to the
front and shook her finger at Piggy.

"How dare you!" she said. "Now you
will get what you deserve."

"Yes he will, ma'am," said Detective Paw. "And you will get every penny of your money back."

Then Patrol Officer Prickles bundled Piggy into his latest police-issue Arrester car.

Back at Big City Police Headquarters, Piggy was put behind bars.

"Good work," said Patrol Officer Prickles.

"I couldn't have done it without you," said Detective Paw.

Detective Paw had a cup of coffee and finished his doughnut. Patrol Officer Prickles had a strawberry-almond milkshake and a banana.

It had been a difficult case, but together they cracked it, and Big City was a little bit safer thanks to Patrol Officer Prickles and Detective Paw.